Dear Parents,

 As the creator of ( the founder of **Dream Big Toy Company,** I would like to thank you for giving your child the gifts of reading and healthy life-skills.

 Healthy habits start early. I created **Go! Go! Sports Girls** as a fun and educational way to promote self-appreciation and the benefits of daily exercise, smart eating and sleeping habits, self-esteem, and overall healthy life-skills for girls. Author Kara Douglass Thom and illustrator Pamela Seatter have taken this dream a step further by creating a series of fun and educational books to accompany the dolls. Now your child can **Read & Play.**

 The books have been written for the child who has begun to read alone, and younger children will enjoy having the stories read to them.

 I believe every child should have the opportunity to **Dream Big and Go For It!**


Sincerely,

*Jodi Bondi Norgaard*

Jodi Bondi Norgaard

*For our very own sports girls*
*Grace, McKenna, Kendall, Jocie Claire,*
*Kaelie, Maia, and Michaela,*
*and their brothers Peter, Ben, Blake,*
*and Alex, who inspire us every day.*
*— JBN, KDT, PS, SRB*

First published in 2014

Series Editor: Susan Rich Brooke

Text © 2014 by Kara Douglass Thom

Illustrations © 2014 by Pamela Seatter

**www.gogosportsgirls.com**

Library of Congress Control Number:  2013951460

First Edition

8 7 6 5 4 3 2 1

This book was printed in 2015 at Luk Ka Packaging Co., Ltd.
in Street No. 98, Lijia Road, Henggang, Longgang Dictrict,
Shenzhen, Guangdong, China.

ISBN 978-1-940731-05-6

# Cheerleader Girl Roxy's Story

## Leading the Way

Written by Kara Douglass Thom

Illustrated by Pamela Seatter

Dream Big Toy Company™

We all have something to cheer about. There's the big stuff, like an A+ on my spelling test or a cavity-free dentist visit. I cheer for little things too, like strawberry waffles for breakfast or a penny on the sidewalk.

I come from a family of cheerleaders. My mom was a cheerleader—and she thinks she still is. When she wants me to get in the car, she chants:

*"Let's GO! Let's GO!*
*L - E - T - S - G - O!"*

My big sister Kaylie is a high-school cheerleader. She's kind, smart, and so pretty. She can do a back flip. And she gets to wear her cheer uniform to school on game days.

I want to be just like her.

As soon as I was old enough, I went to some cheerleading camps. Next I tried out for the youth cheerleading squad. My squad peps up the fans at football games and basketball games. We also go to cheer competitions, where we perform routines in front of judges.

Wherever we go, we always show our spirit. I love to wear my purple cheer uniform and shake my yellow poms.

"Go! Fight! Win!"

That's my favorite cheer.

## Cheer Through the Years

### 1898:
The first cheerleader was a student at the University of Minnesota named Johnny Campbell. That first cheer was: *"Rah, rah, rah! Ski-U-Mah! Varsity, varsity, Minn-e-so-tah!"* For the next 25 years, all cheerleaders were boys.

### 1923:
Girls began cheerleading. But there were still more boy cheerleaders than girl cheerleaders until the 1940s.

### 1930s:
Cheerleaders started using pom-pons, which were made out of paper.

### 1965:
Fred Gastoff created the first poms made of thin strips of plastic.

### 1980s:
Cheerleading began to include dance, gymnastics, and stunts. Cheer competitions turned cheerleading into a sport.

### 2004:
The International Cheer Union was founded, becoming the world governing body of cheerleading, an important step to becoming an Olympic sport.

When the new season started this year,
I tried out for the squad again. Even though
I was on the team last year, I still had to work
hard and do my best to get picked. At the end
of tryouts, the judges announced the new squad.
Everyone from last year was back.

One new girl made the team, too.
Her name was Sophie.

At our first practice, Coach called us together. "I want to make sure everyone has met Sophie," Coach said. "Sophie and her family just moved into town. Let's welcome her to our squad."

We all looked around. Sophie was sitting behind us with her arms wrapped around her long legs. We hadn't even noticed she was there.

We stood up and clapped our hands as we shouted:
"*H - E - double L - O!*
*That's the way we spell HELLO!*
*From up above and down below,*
*We welcome Sophie to our show!*"

"Thanks," Sophie whispered.

We didn't practice chants or cheers that day. Instead, Coach had us play games so we could "get to know each other" and "learn how to work together." We learned a little bit about Sophie, like where she had moved from and how many brothers and sisters she had. But we didn't learn anything about what kind of cheerleader she was.

At the next practice, we taught Sophie one of our chants from last year. She learned the words fast. The trouble was the way she said them. Cheerleaders have to yell, and they all have to yell at the exact same time.

Sophie just couldn't get her words to sound sharp. Her voice was soft, and it trailed off after each word. So she was still saying them after the rest of us finished.

# Words of Cheer

**Chant:** A few words that are repeated, with simple arm movements.

**Cheer:** Words that are set to a routine, which might include movements, dancing, and tumbling.

**Jump:** Some common jumps for cheerleaders are called the toe touch, tuck, hurdler, pike, and herkie.

**Stunt:** An acrobatic trick. Two or more cheerleaders stay on the ground as "bases" to support the "flyers," who jump up in the air.

Ava

Roxy

Sophie

That night at dinner, I told my mom and sister about Sophie. "She's just not getting it," I said, poking my fork around my pile of peas.

"Hmmm," Mom said. "I think you might have forgotten what it's like to be the new girl on the squad. As I recall, you needed a lot of help when you started, too."

"We all have to start somewhere," Kaylie said. "Mom, remember when I tried out for the middle-school cheer team?"

"You were so sad when you couldn't get the arm movements right," Mom said. "I thought you might give up. But look at you now."

"Roxy, do you know how I became a good cheerleader?" Kaylie asked.

I shrugged. I thought she was born the best cheerleader in the world.

"Because good cheerleaders took the time to help me."

Then my mom broke out into a cheer:

*"You've got the power!*
*You've got the soul!*
*You've got the spirit*
*to accomplish your goal!"*

Our next practice didn't go so well. I saw Olivia and Ava give each other worried looks after every cheer. I kept thinking Sophie would get it on the next try, but she never did. By the end of practice, the whole squad was on edge.

One by one, everyone left—except Sophie. She stayed and kept working on the chant. I could tell that she really wanted to get it right. I stayed and watched her.

Then I remembered what my sister said about helping.

"Sophie," I said, "let's practice together."

"OK," she said quietly.

# Tips from the Team

Cheerleaders need to be LOUD. Take deep breaths and use a deeper voice while you cheer. Let the yell come from your chest, not your throat.

If you mess up in front of a crowd, keep smiling until you get back on track. The audience will see your smile, not your mistake.

You need a lot of power to jump high. To avoid injury, bend your knees when your feet hit the ground. This will give you a soft landing.

"Here's something my sister taught me," I said. "Put your hands on your tummy and take a big breath. Do you feel your tummy rise as you breathe in? That's the place where your voice needs to come from. If you yell from your throat, you won't be loud enough."

"*Gooooo!*" Sophie yelled.

"That was good and loud. But you have to make the word sound sharp and short, too. *Go!*"

"*Go!*" Sophie repeated.

"Great. Now let's do the whole chant."

With our fists on our hips, we yelled, "*Go!*"

We extended our arms out to our sides and yelled, "*Fight!*"

Then we raised our arms over our heads and yelled, "*Win!*" Except Sophie said, "*Wiiiiin...*"

"Good try," I said.

"I think I need to practice more," she whispered.

On Saturday night, Olivia invited everyone on the cheer squad to her house for a sleepover. Well, everyone except Sophie.

We listened to music and gave each other crazy hairdos. After a handstand contest to see who could stay up the longest (Maya), Olivia said, "How will we ever be ready for competition?"

"We need to give Sophie time," M.C. said. "Take it from me, learning new things can take a while."

"But we don't have a lot of time," Olivia said. "What if she can't learn our cheer?"

The room grew quiet. What *would* we do if Sophie couldn't learn it? Then my sister's words came back to me again.

"She *will* learn it, because *we're* going to help her," I said. "Remember when I first started cheering? Olivia, without your help, I would never have learned the difference between a bucket and a blade."

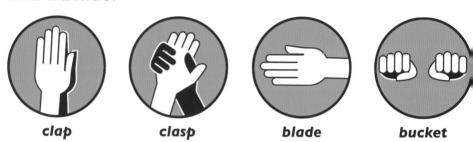

clap          clasp          blade          bucket

"But Roxy," Olivia said, "even if Sophie learns our cheers, she's so...quiet. It's a little weird."

"*I'm* weird," I said. "Look, the birthmark on the back of my leg looks like a koala bear."

"I'm afraid of heights," Maya added.

Gracie stepped up next. "I still sleep with my favorite stuffed animal."

"Mine's weirder," said M.C. "I have an imaginary friend—and he's an elephant."

Ava pulled back her hair. "See my ears? One sticks out more than the other."

"All right, I'll go," Olivia said. "I love vegetables. Even Brussels sprouts. I know. It's totally weird."

"See, we're all a little weird," I said. "That's what makes us interesting."

The more we helped her, the better Sophie got. Her voice became louder and sharper. When she had trouble putting the words together with the movements, we helped her with that, too. Coach reminded her that even if she made a mistake, she needed to smile and keep going.

One day during a break, Maya said, "Let's have a handstand contest!"

"You always win those," Gracie said. "Let's have a jumping contest instead."

"Toe touch," said Olivia. "Me first!"

Each of us jumped, until Sophie was the only one left.

"Your turn, Sophie," I said. "Can you do a toe touch?"

Sophie nodded. Then she sprang so high off the floor we had to raise our heads to see her up in the air. Her toes went up even higher than her hands.

Ava's jaw dropped open. "Where did you learn to jump like that?"

"Practice," said Sophie, and she wasn't even whispering. "I can show you how."

With Coach's help, we put together a cheer routine that showed off everyone's special skills. We helped Sophie cheer with a loud, strong voice, and she helped the rest of us jump higher than we ever thought we could.

"Now *that's* what it means to work together," Coach said. "When you use everyone's strengths, the whole squad will shine."

"We have an awesome cheer routine," Ava said proudly.

## Cheer Gear

**Do wear:**
Shorts, a t-shirt, and comfortable cross-training shoes for practice. A team uniform for games and competitions. A hair band to keep your hair out of your eyes and off your your shoulders.

**Don't wear:**
Baggy clothes or jewelry. And never chew gum when you cheer!

Finally the day came for our first competition! I looked at the audience. Kaylie held up a sign that said, "Lead the Way, Purple Power!" My mom pulled out her old megaphone and yelled, *"Go, Roxy, Go!"*

Sophie and I looked at each other and smiled. I took a deep breath, and we began.

*"The purple team is here!*
*Stand up and cheer!*
*Yell GO! Yell FIGHT! Yell WIN!"*

Our team moved together, and our voices sounded like one. For our final position, Gracie and I kneeled in the middle of the stage. Sophie stepped up on our thighs. Then she sprang up high in the air as we yelled:

*"GO! FIGHT! WIN!"*

When we finished cheering for the audience, the audience started cheering for us!

To celebrate, Ava had a sleepover for the whole squad—including our new friend Sophie.

M.C. won the dance contest. Olivia won the vegetable-eating contest. Maya won the handstand contest (again). And Sophie won the jumping contest (of course).

That night, we all had something to cheer about. I think Sophie cheered the loudest!

# Here's What Roxy Learned:

- Being a leader means doing what you think is right and setting a good example.

- Differences make people interesting. Be proud of what makes you different!

- We all have to start somewhere. Help others when you can.

- Everyone has a strength or talent. When team members work together and use their special talents, the whole team will shine.

# Cheerleader Girl Roxy's Healthy Tips:

- **Warm up.** Cheerleaders need to warm up their bodies *and* their voices. Before practice, Roxy jumps rope and touches her toes. Then she sings: *do re mi fa sol la ti do!*

- **Fuel in.** Natural snacks like oranges or almonds give you more energy than sugary snacks.

- **Drink up.** To replace the water you lose when you sweat, make sure you drink water, not sodas or sugary drinks. Water will also keep your vocal cords moist.

- **Lights out.** Get lots of sleep every night. Cheerleaders need energy to pep up the crowd!

## Dream Big and Go For It!